Night on the Milky Way Railroad

Kenji Miyazawa

Translated by
Shelley Marshall

Shelley Marshall

Copyright © 2022 by Shelley Marshall

ISBN 978-1-959002-02-4

All rights reserved.

No part of this book may be reproduced in any form or by any electronic or mechanical means, including information storage and retrieval systems, without written permission from the author, except for the use of brief quotations in a book review.

www.jpopbooks.com

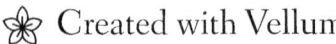 Created with Vellum

Chapter 1
Afternoon Class

"Class, this is called a river, a river that flows with milk. Do you know what this cloudy whiteness is?" asked the teacher pointing at a section that resembled a galactic belt, a blurry whiteness from the top to the bottom in the large, black star chart dangling from the blackboard.

Campanella raised his hand. Soon four or five more hands shot up. Giovanni was about to raise his but stopped. He was sure those were the stars he had read about in a magazine. But Giovanni had been drowsy in class every day. He had no time to read the book and no book to read. He didn't feel he understood much.

But the teacher was quick and caught him.

"Giovanni, you know what this is. Don't you?"

Giovanni hopped up, but anyone who saw him standing there knew he couldn't answer. Zanelli, who sat in front of him, couldn't suppress his laughter when he turned to look. The flustered Giovanni blushed a bright red. Again, the teacher asked, "If you observed a galaxy through a large telescope, what would you mainly see?"

Stars, of course, thought Giovanni, but couldn't bring himself to answer this question right away.

The teacher soon became frustrated and looked at Campanella and called on him.

"Campanella?"

Campanella eagerly raised his hand but hesitantly stood up, and, in the end, couldn't answer.

Night on the Milky Way Railroad

Surprised, the teacher stared at Campanella for a moment and then pointed at the star chart.

"All right. If you look at this dim white galaxy through a powerful telescope, you would see many small stars. Isn't that right, Giovanni?"

Giovanni flushed and nodded as his eyes filled with tears. He knew the answer, and Campanella knew, too. He read about galaxies in a magazine at Campanella's house; his father is a professor. When they finished reading the article, Campanella rushed to get a large book from his father's study and opened the page about the Milky Way. They stared for a long time at the beautiful photograph of a jet-black page filled with white dots. Although Campanella had not forgotten, he did not answer right away. Giovanni had to work in the mornings and afternoons. He went to school but didn't play rowdily with the others and barely spoke to Campanella. Aware of his friend's situation, Campanella did not answer on purpose, out of kindness.

The teacher said, "Well, if you believe that this river in the sky is truly a river, each of these small stars is a cluster of sand or small pebbles in that river. And if you believe the river to be an immense flow of milk, then it would more closely resemble the Milky Way. That is, all of these stars are round, fine, floating balls of fat in milk.

"If that's the case, my next question is what are the waters of this river? The answer is a vacuum in which light travels at a particular speed, and where the Sun and the Earth float. We live in these waters of the Milky Way.

"Look in all directions from the waters of the Milky Way and you can see many stars gathered together in the deep places where the bottom of the Milky Way is far away. This is exactly like when deep water looks bluer. Here, it appears as a white blur. Now, let's take a look at this model."

The teacher pointed to a large two-sided convex lens containing many grains of twinkling sand inside.

"The Milky Way is formed like this.

Night on the Milky Way Railroad

Each twinkling grain is believed to be a shining star just like our sun. The sun is nearly at the center, and the Earth is very close to it. At night, you are standing at this center and looking around inside this lens. There are few twinkling grains in this direction because the lens is thin. In other words, you'll see few stars.

"On the other hand, the glass is thick here and here, so you can see many twinkling grains, namely the stars. The distant ones look like dim white blurs. Well, this concludes today's discussion of the Milky Way. We're out of time. In the next science lesson, we'll discuss the size of this lens and the variety of stars inside.

"Tonight is the Milky Way festival, everyone should go outside and take a close look at the Milky Way. Now, please put away your books and notes."

The room filled with the sounds of desktops opening and closing, and books being stacked. A short time later, everyone stood at attention, bowed to the teacher, and left the classroom.

Chapter 2
The Printer's Shop

Giovanni walked out the school gate to see seven or eight of his classmates gathered around Campanella. Instead of going home, he was at the cherry blossom tree in a corner of the school grounds. They seemed to be talking about making blue lamps out of gourds to bring to the star festival tonight and float down the river.

Giovanni gave them a big wave and walked out the school gate. Balls made from yew trees hung outside the houses in town. Lamps swung from cypress tree branches. These were some of the many decorations for the night's Milky Way festival.

Giovanni didn't go home but turned three corners to finally arrive at a large printer's shop. He took off his shoes and went in. He opened a large door at the end of a hallway. It was still daytime, but the lights were on inside. Amid the churning of many rotary printing presses, men wearing bandannas or light shades read and counted aloud as they worked and sounded like they were singing.

Giovanni bowed to the man seated at the third high table from the entrance. After searching the shelves for a short time, the man handed him a scrap of paper.

"Here, get these."

Giovanni picked up a small shallow box at the foot of the man's table, went over to the corner of a propped-up wall with many electric lights attached, crouched down, and began picking up one tiny type, about the size of a millet seed, after another with small tweezers. A man wearing a blue printer's bib passed behind Giovanni and said, "Good afternoon, Mr. Magnifying Glasses."

Without making a sound or looking at him, four or five people nearby laughed coldly.

Giovanni picked up the types one by one, often rubbing his eyes.

A little after six that evening, for the last time, Giovanni compared the sheet of paper he held in his hand with the letters he picked up and placed in the small box. He took the box to the man at the table. Without a word, the man took the box and gave a slight nod.

Giovanni bowed, then opened the door and went over to the register. Without a word, a man wearing white clothes handed him one small silver coin. Giovanni perked up and gave a smart bow.

He picked up his bag under the machine and dashed out to the street. Whistling lively, he made a beeline to the bakery. He bought a loaf of bread, a bag of sugar cubes, and raced out.

Chapter 3
Home

Giovanni was full of life when he returned home, a small house in a back street. Purple kale and asparagus were planted in an open box near the leftmost of three entrances. The sunshades were pulled down over two small windows.

"Mom, I'm home. Are you feeling better?" asked Giovanni, as he removed his shoes.

"Oh, Giovanni, hello. You're probably tired from work. It was cool today. I felt fine all day."

As Giovanni stepped up from the entryway, his mother was resting, covered with a white cloth. Giovanni opened the windows.

"Mom, I bought sugar cubes today. I'll put them in milk for you."

"You should drink some first. I don't want any yet."

"Mom, when did Sis come home?"

"Around three. She made all the food over there."

"No one delivered your milk, did they?"

"No, they didn't."

"I'll go and get it."

"You eat first while I rest. Sis can make anything from tomatoes. She put it over there."

"Then I'll have some."

Giovanni took a plate of tomatoes to a window and gobbled up the tomatoes with bread.

"Hey, Mom. I think Dad's coming home soon."

"So do I. But why do you think so?"

"Well, today's paper said that fishing up north was great this year."

"Yes, but your father probably isn't fishing."

"I'm sure he is. Dad wouldn't do anything bad and get thrown in jail. The giant crab shell and reindeer antlers he gave to the school are stored in the specimen room. The sixth-grade teachers pass them around in class."

"The sea otter coat from your father came."

"Everyone will say I look nice in it, but they'll be making fun of me."

"They tease you?"

"Yes, but not Campanella. He doesn't say anything mean. Campanella feels bad for me when the others say those kinds of things."

"Campanella's father and your father were friends since they were little, just like you two."

"Oh, so that's why Dad took me to Campanella's house. We had fun that time. Sometimes on the way home from school, I stop by his house.

"He has a train powered by an alcohol

lamp. We put the seven tracks together to make a circle. The set also has telegraph poles and signals. The train only passes through when the signal light is green. One time, the alcohol ran out, so we used oil, but the boiler got all sooty."

"Is that so?"

"I deliver their newspaper every morning. Now, it's always quiet at that house."

"Well, it's still early."

"They have a dog named Sauer. His tail is like a broom. When I leave, he comes with me sniffing all the way to the edge of town. Sometimes, he goes even further. Tonight, everybody's going to float gourd lamps on the river. I'm sure that dog will be there, too."

"Oh. The Milky Way festival's tonight."

"Yes, I'm going to have a look when I go get the milk."

"You may go but don't go in the river."

"Okay, I'll only watch from the river bank. I'll be back in an hour."

"Go and have fun. If you're with Campanella, I won't worry."

Night on the Milky Way Railroad

"Yes, we'll definitely go together. Mom, should I close the window?"

"Yes, please. It's a little chilly."

Giovanni closed the window. After he straightened up the dishes and the bread bag, he nearly jumped into his shoes and flew out the dark doorway.

"I'll be back in an hour and a half."

Chapter 4
Night of the Centaur Festival

Giovanni looked sad. His pouting mouth looked like he was whistling. He left town down a hill covered by the blackness of lines of cypress trees.

At the bottom of the hill, a large street lamp radiated a splendid bluish-white light. As Giovanni slowly approached the street lamp, his long dark shadow stretched behind him like a phantom slowly darkening to jet black. He raised his legs and waved his hands to look like they wrapped around to his side.

Giovanni took big steps past the bottom

of the street lamp and imagined, I'm an awesome locomotive speeding down a hill. Now I'm rushing past the street lamp. My shadow is a compass. I'll go around there and end up in front.

His classmate Zanelli wearing a new shirt with a pointed collar popped out of a small dark alley on the other side of the street lamp and brushed passed him.

Giovanni asked, "Zanelli, are you going to float gourds on the river?"

Zanelli yelled back, "Giovanni, did you get that sea otter coat from your father?"

Giovanni, ears ringing like he was punched, yelled back, "What did you say, Zanelli?"

Unfortunately, he had already disappeared into the house with *hinoki* plants across the street.

He wondered, Why does Zanelli say things like that to me when I haven't done anything to him? He always runs away like a rat, out of habit. He's just a jerk for saying things like that to me when I haven't done anything.

Giovanni walked down the street decorated with lamps and tree branches. Many thoughts raced through his head. The clock shop had bright neon lights. The red eyes of an owl made of stone spun around each second. Various jewels were set on a thick glass plate colored like the ocean and rotated slowly like stars, and a copper man and horse slowly inched around from the far side.

A black planisphere at the center was decorated with blue asparagus leaves. Giovanni was lost in thought as he gazed at this map of the constellations. It was a very small copy of the map he had seen that day in school.

The plate is turned to match a particular date and time. The sky matching destined to emerge at that time appears to move in an ellipse. As expected, running vertically down the center, the Milky Way appears as a dim, fuzzy belt that looks as if faint explosions were billowing up from the bottom.

Behind it, a small telescope on a tripod

stood in yellowish light. A large chart pinned to the back wall depicted the constellations in the sky in the shapes of a beast, a snake, a fish, and a jar.

Giovanni daydreamed about whether the scorpion, the hero, and all the others were really so close in the sky, and wanted to see how far he could walk among them. He suddenly remembered the milk for his mother and left the store.

The slight tightness around his coat's shoulders bothered him, but Giovanni stood tall and passed through town swinging his arms like he was on a mission.

Crisp, clear air flowed like water through the streets and into the stores. The street lamps were wrapped with decorative branches of fir and oak trees. Many small lights hung from the six sycamore trees in front of the electric company. It was the image of a mermaid city.

Children in their new creased kimonos delighted in playing the song *Hoshi Meguri, The Star Journey*, on their whistles, chanting "Centaurus, send us dewdrops" in a plea for life-giving water, and lighting up blue magnesia sparklers. Burdened by thoughts far from the spirited fun and games, Giovanni's head hung low in his rush to the milk dealer.

A little while later, Giovanni came to a part of town where poplar trees floated high in the starry sky. He entered the black gate of the dairy and stood in front of a dark kitchen surrounded by the weak aroma of cows. He removed his hat and said, "Good evening."

The house was quiet. No one seemed to be there.

Giovanni stood up straight and again said, "Good evening. Is anybody here?"

A few moments later, a sickly-looking old woman, slowly shuffled in and asked what he wanted.

Giovanni earnestly said, "Hello, no one delivered my milk today. Could I get it now?"

"No one is here who can help you. Come back tomorrow," she said while rubbing her reddened eyes.

Giovanni lowered his eyes.

"My mother is sick. So if it wouldn't be too much trouble, could I get it tonight?"

"Come back a little later, please," she said and walked away.

"Oh, okay. Thank you," said Giovanni, then he bowed and left the kitchen.

Giovanni turned the corner of an intersection in town and saw a jumble of black shadows and blurry white shirts of six or seven students in front of the general store across the bridge. They were coming toward him blowing whistles and laughing. Everyone was carrying a gourd lamp.

Those laughing voices and whistles sounded familiar. They were his classmates. Giovanni almost turned back automatically but changed his mind and walked toward them with a spring in his step.

Giovanni was about to ask if they were going to the river but after a little thought, choked up. Then he heard Zanelli shout, "Giovanni, you got your sea otter coat."

Everyone immediately joined in and

also yelled, "Giovanni, you got your sea otter coat."

Giovanni turned bright red, tried to look like he didn't hear them, and quickly walked by. Campanella was in the group but said nothing. He laughed a little but looked miserable and glanced at Giovanni to see if he was mad.

Giovanni avoided his gaze. Soon Campanella's tall figure passed by and everyone was again blowing a simple song on their whistles.

At the corner, he turned around to look back and caught Zanelli looking back at him. Campanella was blowing a loud whistle and walking toward the dim, distant bridge. Words could not describe Giovanni sorrow and loneliness.

He sprinted off. Small children were skipping on one leg, giggling, and covering their ears with their hands. They thought Giovanni was funny and squealed with joy.

Giovanni dashed off and came to a black hill in no time.

Chapter 5
The Pillar of the Wheel of Heaven

On the far side of the pasture was a low hill. Above its black, flat summit, the Great Bear Constellation looked slightly lower than usual.

Giovanni slowly climbed a path in a small woods already covered in dew. In the pitch-black grass and bamboo thicket that appeared to change its shape, a ray of white starlight lit a small path.

Tiny bugs twinkled blue lights in the grass. Some leaves glowed a faint transparent blue that reminded Giovanni of the gourd lamps everyone had been carrying.

The empty sky suddenly opened beyond these pitch-black pine and oak trees and the Milky Way emerged from the south and extended to the north. The top resembled the Pillar of the Wheel of Heaven, that summons the dead.

As Giovanni climbed, flowers on one side, perhaps balloon flowers or wild chrysanthemums, opened like in a dream to release their scents while a singing bird flew over the hill.

Giovanni reached the summit at the bottom of the Pillar of the Wheel of Heaven and threw himself onto the cold grass.

Lights from the town engulfed by blackness shined brightly like the scene of a shrine at the bottom of the sea. He could still hear the singing and whistling children and distant snatches of shouts. The wind sounded far off and the grass on the hill gently rustled. Giovanni was chilled by his cold shirt soaked in sweat.

He heard the sound of a train coming from the field. A line of small red windows of a small train came into view. In the windows, he thought he glimpsed many passengers engaged in activities like peeling apples and laughing. He felt a sadness beyond words and again looked at the sky.

[*Five missing pages in the original*]

No matter how long he looked, he couldn't believe that the sky was the empty, cold place described by the teacher that afternoon. The longer he looked, he couldn't help thinking that there were small forests and pastures or fields.

Giovanni blinked at the dazzling blue Lyra constellation split into three or four parts and saw the legs extend and draw back many times. They seemed to lengthen like a mushroom. From here, the town looked more like an enormous collection of obscure stars or a massive cloud of smoke to Giovanni.

Chapter 6
Milky Way Station

Giovanni watched the Pillar of the Wheel of Heaven directly behind him fade into a fuzzy pyramidal signal tower and soon blinked like a firefly. It slowly transformed, becoming more distinct, and ultimately no longer moved in a dark steel-blue field in the sky. The object stood upright in this field in the sky like a newly fired blue steel plate.

A mysterious voice from out of nowhere announced, "Milky Way Station. Milky Way Station."

Suddenly, a light flashed brightly in

Night on the Milky Way Railroad

front of him, like lights from a billion firefly squids instantly fossilized and dropped down into the sky. Giovanni reacted by rubbing his eyes vigorously as the light brightened before him. It was like someone suddenly upset and scattered all the diamonds a diamond company pretended not to have mined and hidden them away in a scam to fix a high price.

When he regained his senses, the small train Giovanni was riding still chugged along. In fact, Giovanni was riding in a car for the night-service light rail lined with small yellow electric lights. He peered out the window he sat next to.

The benches covered in blue velvet in the compartment were mostly empty. Reflections of two large brass buttons shined on the far wall varnished to a mousy brown.

Giovanni noticed a tall boy wearing a wet black overcoat sitting in the seat in front of him. The boy was sticking his head out of the window and looking around.

A strange feeling overcame him as he stared at the boy's shoulders for a long time. For some reason, Giovanni really wanted to know who he was. Just as Giovanni was about to stick his head out of his window, the boy pulled his head back in and looked at Giovanni.

It was Campanella. Before Giovanni asked Campanella if he had been there all along, Campanella said, "Everyone was running fast but fell behind. Zanelli was running fast, too, but couldn't catch up."

While thinking, Oh, so we're still invited to go together, Giovanni asked, "Are they waiting for us somewhere?"

Campanella said, "Zanelli's already gone home. His father came to get him."

Giovanni wondered why Campanella was talking that way, he seemed troubled and his face looked a little pale. A hunch told Giovanni something was wrong as if he had forgotten something somewhere.

While peering out of the window, Campanella seemed to get better and said with some spirit, "Oh shoot, I forgot the water flask...and my sketchbook. But it doesn't really matter. We'll soon be at Swan Depot. I'd really like to see the swans. I'll definitely be able to see them flying beyond the river."

Campanella studied a map printed on a round board and was turning it round and round. On the map, the white streak of a railroad line along the left bank of the Milky Way traced a path to the south.

The best parts of the map were the stations, the signal towers, and the ponds and forests sparkling in beautiful blue, orange, and green lights on the board, pitch black like the night. Giovanni wondered what kind of map it was and where he had seen it.

Giovanni asked, "Where did you buy that map? It's made of obsidian, isn't it?"

"I got it at Milky Way Station. Did you get one?"

"Well, I'll probably pass through Milky Way Station. We're probably around here now," said Giovanni and pointed north of the depot sign reading Swan. Looking north, Giovanni said, "Oh, I see. That shore may be a moonlit night." Silver pampas grass in the sky on the bank of the Milky Way glowing in a blue-white light gently rustled in a breeze like standing waves. "No, that's not a moonlit night. It's twinkling because it's the Milky Way," said Giovanni.

He felt happy like he wanted to leap up and stomp his feet. He stuck his head out the window and stretched with all his might while whistling *The Star Journey* as loud as he could. He gazed at the waters of the Milky Way. At first, they were a little blurry. He slowly realized those beautiful waters, more transparent than glass or hydrogen, flowed silently like the glimmering, fine purple-colored waves radiating like a rainbow. From time to time, he squinted as the silent waters crept closer.

Enchanting phosphorescent signal towers gracefully dotted the fields. The signal towers in the faraway fields were smaller, and the closer ones were bigger. The towers were yellowish-orange in the distance and tinted bluish-white close-up. The scene was filled with a variety of glimmering fields, triangular or rectangular resembling zigzags or chains.

Giovanni was so excited, he shook his head in amazement. Those beautiful, glittering, blue and orange signal towers in the fields were breathtaking and seemed to quiver as if each one was breathing.

Giovanni said, "I already went to a field in the sky," and added, "This train probably doesn't carry coal," while sticking out his left hand and looking out the window toward the front.

"The train probably runs on alcohol or electricity," said Campanella.

Immediately, a voice sounding like a cello boomed out the answer from somewhere far off in the haze.

"This train doesn't run on steam nor electricity. It simply runs because it has decided to run. You thought you heard rattling sounds, but those are merely the train sounds you're used to hearing."

"I heard that voice many times somewhere."

"I've heard it many times in the forest and by the river."

The splendid little train chugged along to a destination somewhere in the fluttering winds of the silver pampas grass in the sky and in the waters of the Milky Way or in the dim bluish-white lights at the three vertices of some triangle.

"Oh, the flowers on the path through the woods are blooming. It's definitely fall," said Campanella pointing out the window.

Amazing purple flowers along the path resembling engravings in moonstone were blooming in the small grassy field at the edge of the track.

Giovanni was enchanted.

"Can't I jump off, pick a few, then hop back on?"

Before Campanella could finish saying, "That's a bad idea. You'll be left far behind," they came up to gleaming flowers at

Night on the Milky Way Railroad

the next path. One after the other, many flower cups with yellow bottoms on the paths passed before their eyes, bubbling and gushing out like pouring rain. The line of signal towers glimmered and glittered more and more like blazing fires.

Chapter 7
The Northern Cross and the Pliocene Coastline

Campanella hurriedly and with a slight stutter said, "Mother, can you forgive me?"

Giovanni vaguely thought, Oh, I get it. My mother is near that orange signal tower in the distance visible like a spot of dust and is thinking about me.

"I'll do anything to truly make my mother happy. What would make her the happiest?" asked Campanella trying his best not to cry.

He didn't know why, but Giovanni yelled, "Your mother isn't bad."

"I don't understand. But if someone did

something really good, you would be happiest, right? So I think my mother will understand," said Campanella who appeared resolute.

Suddenly, a bright white light filled the interior of the train car. Amorphous water silently flowed above the riverbed of the gorgeous Milky Way that gathered all of the splendidness of diamonds and dew on the grass.

An island with a faint bluish-white halo could be seen inside the flow. A splendid, astonishing white cross stood on the flat summit of the island. It may have been cast in the clouds of the frozen North Pole or has silently stood forever giving off an invigorating golden light.

"Hallelujah! Hallelujah!" rose voices in front and behind the boys. When they turned to look, all of the travelers in the car had stood. They were clutching black Bibles to their breasts and holding crystal prayer beads, some had clasped their humble fingers together and were praying.

Without thinking, Giovanni and Campanella jumped to their feet. Campanella's cheeks seemed to glow red like ripe apples.

The island and the cross slowly faded behind them.

The far bank also shimmered as a dim, pale light, and sometimes resembled pampas grass fluttering in the wind. In an instant, silver smoke appeared and resembled breathing. The grasses hiding behind then emerging from the many flowers along the path in the forest reminded them of jack o'lanterns.

In moments, the space between the river and the train was blocked by a line of pampas grass. Looking back just twice, Swan Island was faraway and small and seemed to turn into a painting. The pampas grass rustled and eventually could no longer be seen.

Behind Giovanni, a tall Catholic nun dressed in black who had boarded some time ago immediately lowered her perfectly round, green eyes and appeared to be humbly listening to some words or a voice.

The travelers quietly returned to their seats.

Giovanni and Campanella, who both felt a new feeling resembling sorrow filling their hearts, halfheartedly spoke to each other in hushed voices.

"We'll soon arrive at Swan Depot."

"Yes, we'll get there at exactly eleven o'clock."

They caught a glimpse of a green signal lamp and a dim white pillar passing outside the window. Then a soft, hazy light resembling a sulfur flame in front of the track switch passed below their window. The train slowed down. A line of lamps along the platform appeared in a beautiful regular pattern and steadily increased in size and breadth. When the train stopped, the boys were in front of the huge clock at the Swan Depot.

On the clock panel illustrating an invigorating autumn scene, two clock hands made of blue-fired steel pointed to exactly eleven o'clock. Everyone disembarked quickly and left the car deserted.

"'Train departs in 20 minutes" was written below the clock.

"Should we get off and look around?" asked Giovanni.

"Yeah, let's get off."

The boys jumped up together, flew out the door, and took off for the ticket gate. But at the gate, only one bright purple lamp was lit. No one was there. They looked around but didn't see a station manager, a porter, or even a shadow.

The boys went to a small plaza in front of the depot enclosed by ginkgo trees that looked like creations made of crystal.

A wide street extended from the plaza into the blue phosphorescence of the Milky Way.

No matter where they went, they didn't see one person who had gotten off the train before them. As the boys walked side by side down this white street, their shadows fell in all directions like the spokes of two wheels, or like the shadows of two pillars in a room with windows on all sides.

Soon they came to the gorgeous shore they saw from the train.

Campanella pointed to a pinch of beautiful sand spread out on the palm of his hand. In a dream-like state, he said, "These sands are crystals. A small fire is burning in each one."

"Really," said Giovanni, not paying attention but wondering where he could learn about things like that.

The pebbles on the shore were crystals, topaz, the elements exposed in the wrinkled folds of mountains, and corundum radiating bluish-white light like mist from ridges. Giovanni ran to the shore and dipped his hands in the water.

The mysterious waters of the Milky Way were more transparent than hydrogen. Nevertheless, the waters appeared as a faintly mercury-colored flow skimming over their hands that both boys submerged up to their wrists. The waves bumping against their wrists radiated a beautiful phosphorescence resembling sparkling flames.

Looking above the river and below the cliffs filled with sprouting pampas grass, they saw a white rock jutting out flat like a playing field along the river. On it stood the small shadows of five or six people who seemed to be digging up or burying something. They were standing up and bending, and tools of some sort glinted randomly.

"Let's go see," the boys shouted in unison and started running. A slick porcelain placard stating *Pliocene Coastline* stood at the entrance to the white rock. At scattered positions on the far-off shore, slender iron railings were erected, and beautiful wooden benches, installed.

"Something's strange," said Campanella who mysteriously stood still. An object like the sharp, slender, black point of walnut fruit extended from the rock.

"That is the fruit of a walnut. There are lots of them. They're flowing toward us, aren't they? They're in the rock."

"They're big, twice the size of walnuts. There are some over there."

"Hurry, let's go see. They are definitely digging up something."

Carrying the jagged black walnut fruits, the boys walked on. The waves approached the shore on the left in a gentle zigzag. On the cliffs to the left, the spikes of the pampas grass that seemed to be made of silver or shells swayed.

They slowly approached and saw a tall, bookish man in boots and wearing very strong eyeglasses for nearsightedness. As he feverishly wrote in a notebook, he was absorbed in giving instructions to three people who looked like his assistants. They brandished pickaxes and gripped shovels.

"Shovel without breaking off the projections. Dig a little deeper. No. No. Why are you so rough?"

Coming from the soft white rocks, they could see more than half of a large, a very large, pale exposed bone of a wild animal that seemed to have fallen on its side and shattered. They noticed a rock with two hoof prints cleanly cut apart into about ten squares, and each section assigned a number.

While cleaning his glasses, the scholarly man asked the boys, "Are you two visitors?"

"There seems to be a lot of walnuts. They may be about 1.2 million years old. Quite young. This place was the coastline during the Tertiary period about 1.2 million years ago, and the shells emerged from under here. Saltwater surged in then receded to where the river flows now.

"This beast, this one is an auroch. Hey! Hey, stop using the pickaxe. Work carefully with a chisel. Yes, the auroch is an ancestor of today's cow. They were plentiful long ago."

"Are you collecting specimens?"

"No, we need proof. Here, we see a thick, rich stratum. It can give us different evidence from about 1.2 million years ago. However, others may wonder what we see in this kind of stratum. They may see it as wind, water, or empty sky. Do you understand? But...Hey! Don't use a shovel there either. There may be ribs buried right beneath you."

The boys trotted alongside the Professor.

Campanella checked his map and wristwatch and said, "It's time. Let's go."

"Well, we have to go. Goodbye," Giovanni politely said to the Professor.

"Really? I mean, goodbye," said the Professor, scurrying around as he returned to supervising.

The boys ran at top speed on the white rock to catch the train. They ran like the wind but didn't run out of breath, and their knees never burned.

Giovanni thought, If we can run like this, we can run all over the world.

The boys passed the shore. Gradually, the lights at the ticket gate grew bigger. In a few moments, they could see the people seated in their car through the windows.

Chapter 8
The Bird Catcher

"May I sit here?" asked a gruff but kind man's voice from behind the boys.

He was a slightly stooped, red-bearded man and wore a somewhat raggedy brown cloak. On each shoulder, he carried a sack closed shut by a white cloth.

"Yes, it's okay," said Giovanni and slouched a little in greeting. A little smile emerged from under his beard as the man slowly set his sacks on the luggage rack. A pang of sadness hit Giovanni when he silently glanced at the clock face. A tone resembling a glass whistle sounded far ahead of them. The train began to silently move.

Campanella was looking at different places on the ceiling of the car. A black beetle stopped at a light and cast a long shadow on the ceiling. The red-bearded man observed Giovanni and Campanella and laughed with nostalgia. The train accelerated slowly. The lights shining from each passing window illuminated the pampas grass and the river.

The red-bearded man a little hesitantly asked the boys, "Where are you fellows going?"

"As far as we can," answered Giovanni, sounding a bit annoyed.

"That's good. This train can take you everywhere."

"Where're you going?" bluntly asked Campanella like he was picking a fight. This made Giovanni burst out laughing. The man seated across the aisle glanced at them laughing, too. He wore a pointed hat and a large key dangled from his belt. Campanella turned red and laughed. The red-

bearded man didn't get mad. His cheeks quivered when he spoke.
"I'm getting off soon. I trap and sell birds."
"What kind of birds?"
"Cranes, wild geese, herons, and swans."
"Are there a lot of cranes?"
"I've been hearing their cries for a while. Can't you hear them?"
"No."
"You can't even hear them now? Listen very carefully."
The boys looked up and listened. They could hear the rattling vibrations of the train and sounds resembling gushing from the wind blowing through the pampas grass.
"How do you catch a crane?"
"A crane, or a crane and a heron?"
"A heron," said Giovanni but thinking either would be fine.
"It's not hard at all. The sands by the Milky Way harden. The herons can be mesmerized. They always return to the

river, from the source to the end. You simply wait in the dry riverbed and quickly press down where the heron's legs land so they stick to the ground. The heron gets stuck and peacefully dies. You already understand the rest. It's exactly like pressing a leaf."

"The herons are pressed like leaves? Are they specimens?"

"No, they're not specimens. They're eaten."

"That's strange," said Campanella tilting his head.

"It's neither strange nor puzzling," said the man then stood and took a sack off the rack and nimbly untied it.

"Look, I just caught these."

"They are really heron," blurted the boys. The herons' bodies glimmered like the pure white Northern Cross they saw earlier. There were only ten. They were a little flattened with shrunken black legs and resembled engravings.

"Their eyes are shut," said Campanella. His fingers touched the heron's closed white eyes shaped like crescent moons. White feathers stuck to their heads like spears.

"Yes, they are," said the bird catcher. He wrapped up the package again in a wrapping cloth and bound it with twine.

Giovanni wondered if you could eat heron on the train and asked, "Does heron taste good?"

"Yes, I get orders for it every day. But I sell more wild geese. Geese look better and are no trouble. Look here," said the bird catcher and untied the other package. Although a little flat, the yellow and bluish-white speckled geese lined up beak to beak glowed like lamps.

"We can eat this now. How about it? Have some," said the bird catcher. He lightly tugged on the yellow leg of a goose. It cleanly broke away like it was made of chocolate.

"How about it? Have some," said the bird catcher, tore the meat in two and handed a piece to each boy.

While eating greedily, Giovanni

thought, What is this? This is candy. Better than chocolate, much better. Does this kind of goose fly? This man is a confectioner from a field somewhere. I feel kind of bad because I was making fun of him before, and now I'm eating his candy.

"Here, have a little more," said the bird catcher and took out another package. Giovanni wanted more but held back and said, "No, thank you."

The bird catcher offered it to the man with the big key across the aisle.

"Thank you, excuse me for taking your merchandise," said the man removing his hat.

"No, you're welcome. How is it? This year the migrating bird business is ..."

"This is great. Around the time of the second limit, the day before yesterday, phone calls came from everywhere asking why the light from the lighthouse was darkened against regulations. But I hadn't done anything.

"The migrating birds gathered close together. And when they passed in front of the light, the sky turned pitch black. There was nothing I could do. I ... the idiots brought me their complaints. I put on my tattered cloak and became an absurd little general from my feet to my mouth. Ha, ha, ha!"

When the pampas grass disappeared, a shining light appeared in a far-off field.

"Why are the heron a problem?" asked Campanella asking the question he had been thinking about for some time.

"The problem is when you eat heron," said the bird catcher turning to look at them.

"They are hung in the water light of the Milky Way for ten days. If not, they must be buried in the sand for three or four days so all of the mercury evaporates, then they can be eaten."

"This isn't a bird. It's candy, right?" Campanella asked boldly. He shared the same thought.

"Well, this is my stop," said the flustered bird catcher. He stood, grabbed his sacks, and disappeared.

Night on the Milky Way Railroad

"Where'd he go?" asked the boys looking at each other. The lighthouse keeper laughed with a grin and stretched a little to glance out the window beside the boys. The boys looked out and saw one side of the shore covered with cottonweed emitting a beautiful yellow and bluish-white phosphorescent light, and the bird catcher who a moment before had been standing next to them. He wore a serious expression as he spread both hands wide and stared intently at the sky.

The boys said, "He's over there. This is really strange. He's definitely going to trap some more birds. I hope the birds come down soon before the train leaves."

From the empty dark violet-colored sky, many herons, like the ones they saw before, squawked *gya-gya* as they gently landed like falling snow. Standing with his legs open at a sixty-degree angle, the delighted bird catcher used both hands to push the shrunken black legs of the falling heron one after another into a cloth sack until he captured the exact number ordered. The herons in the sack blinked blue light like fireflies for a short time, but eventually, they all became dull white and closed their eyes.

The birds he didn't catch, which greatly outnumbered the ones he caught, landed safely on the sands of the Milky Way. Whether their feet stuck or not in the sand, they shrunk and flattened like melting snow, then they spread out on top of the sand and pebbles like copper sap flowing out of a blast furnace. A short time later, the shapes of the birds were impressed into the sand. They lightened and darkened two or three times then turned the same color as their surroundings.

When the bird catcher put twenty birds in the sack, he quickly raised both hands like a soldier who had been hit by a bullet and was about to die. Then, the bird catcher disappeared again.

"Ah, that was refreshing. Isn't it nice to make a living perfect for your body?" said a familiar voice beside Giovanni. He looked and saw the bird catcher perfectly stacking the birds he just caught.

"What?! How did you get from over there to here so fast?" asked Giovanni, confused over what was normal and what was not.

"How? I came because I was about to come. Where did you come from?"

Giovanni expected to answer promptly, but no matter how hard he tried, he could not remember where he came from. Campanella seemed to remember something and blushed.

"Oh, you came from far away," said the bird catcher and gave a quick nod as if he understood.

Chapter 9
Giovanni's Ticket

"This is the Swan District terminal. Look over there. That's the famous Albireo Observatory."

Outside the window, four large black buildings stood in the center of the Milky Way that seemed packed with fireworks. Two dazzling, large transparent balls of blue sapphire and yellow topaz silently went around and around in a ring on one of the flat roofs. As the yellow ball gradually retreated and the small blue ball came forward, the edges of the two balls soon overlapped to form the beautiful green shape of a lens with two convex faces.

Night on the Milky Way Railroad

The center slowly swelled until the blue ball emerged directly in front of the topaz ball to create a green center surrounded by a bright yellow ring. The blue ball then slowly journeyed to the opposite side of the yellow one to reverse the form of the front lens. In time they separated again, and the sapphire ball retreated, and the yellow ball returned again to the front to create the earlier scene.

In reality, this black observatory was quietly lying on its side as though asleep surrounded by the formless, soundless waters of the Milky Way.

The bird catcher explained, "That device measures the velocity of the water. The water also..."

"Tickets, please," interrupted a tall conductor in a red cap and nearly standing at attention beside their seats.

Without a word, the bird catcher took a small piece of paper out of his pocket. The conductor briefly looked at it then turned to Giovanni and Campanella. He stuck out his hand with fingers moving, seeming to ask, "And your tickets?"

"Well," said Giovanni fidgeting. Campanella nonchalantly took out a small gray ticket. Giovanni was completely flustered, but he reached into his coat pocket thinking maybe something was inside, and felt a large folded piece of paper. He quickly took it out as he wondered how it got in there.

It was a green piece of paper about the size of a postcard that had been folded twice. He thought, Jackpot! as he handed the paper to the waiting hand of the conductor. The conductor immediately composed himself and carefully opened and examined the paper. Reading the paper prompted him to earnestly adjust the buttons on his coat. The curious lighthouse keeper peeked at the paper from below. This made Giovanni a little anxious, thinking the paper was some kind of certificate.

"Is this for people from the three-dimensional space?" asked the conductor.

Night on the Milky Way Railroad

"I really don't know," said a relieved Giovanni looking up at the conductor and stifling a laugh but now relieved.

"Very good. We will arrive at the Southern Cross around three o'clock," said the conductor, handed back the paper to Giovanni and left.

An impatient Campanella hurried to see what was on the paper. Giovanni was eager to see, too. One side of the paper was only a strange, single cross printed within a black arabesque pattern. Silently they looked and felt as if they were being drawn to it.

The bird catcher glanced sideways at the paper and said, a little rattled, "Wow! That's a very important document. It's a ticket to go to the true Heaven, if you wish. And not just Heaven, but a pass to go anywhere you want. Whoever holds this, of course, should be able to go anywhere on this Milky Way Railroad in this unfinished fourth dimension dream. You're a V.I.P."

"I understand none of this," said a flushed Giovanni, then he folded up the paper and put it in his pocket. A little embarrassed, he stared out the window again with Campanella but was vaguely aware of the bird catcher glancing at him from time to time as if he were a big shot.

"We'll reach Eagle Depot soon," said Campanella, as he compared a line of three small bluish-white signal towers on the distant coast to the map.

For some reason, Giovanni couldn't help feeling sudden pity for the bird catcher beside him. When he recalled the bird catcher's sheer enjoyment when he caught the herons and wrapped them round and round in white cloth, and his surprise and excitement at seeing the ticket in a side glance, Giovanni thought if only he had something, food, or something he could do, he'd like to truly make the bird catcher, a total stranger, happy. Giovanni sensed the bird catcher would enjoy spending one hundred years standing on the shores of the gleaming Milky Way and catching birds.

Giovanni no longer wanted to be silent

and badly wanted to ask the bird catcher something, but he reconsidered, thinking that would be too abrupt. While he was wondering what to do, the bird catcher vanished. The packages on the wire rack were gone, too.

Maybe, he thought the bird catcher was outside the window with his feet firmly planted and looking at the sky to catch heron, and quickly looked outside. He only saw beautiful sand on one side and waves of pampas grass but not the pointed hat and the broad back of the bird catcher.

"Where'd he go?" asked Campanella, a little distracted. "Where'd he go? And where will we meet him again? Why didn't I talk with him a little more?"

"Yeah, that's what I was thinking, too."

"He was a bit of a nuisance. So I was pretty cold."

Giovanni thought this was the first time he felt this queer feeling. He never said anything like that before.

"Hey, I smell apples. It's probably because I'm thinking about them," said Campanella, looking around baffled.

"No. It really does smell like apples. I smell wild roses, too."

Giovanni also looked around, but the smell seemed to be coming in through the windows. He thought, It's fall so I shouldn't be smelling wild flowers.

Suddenly, a boy of just six with shiny black hair in an unbuttoned red jacket was standing there barefoot, trembling and shivering with a look of astonishment. Next to the boy and tightly holding his hand, a tall young man neatly dressed in a black suit stood like a zelkova tree that had been hit by a blast of wind.

"Wh ... where are we? Oh, what a beautiful place."

Behind the young man was a cute brown-eyed girl of about twelve wearing a black overcoat. She clung to the young man's arm as she looked curiously out the window.

"Oh, this is Lancashire. No ... no, it's Connecticut. No, we have gone into the sky. We have gone to Heaven. Look! That sign is a sign of Heaven. There's nothing to fear anymore. We are being summoned by God," the beaming young man joyously told the girl. But why was his forehead still etched with deep lines, and he seemed so tired? He forced a smile, sat the boy next to Giovanni, and gently pointed the girl to the seat next to Campanella. The girl meekly sat down and neatly folded her hands together.

The boy made a strange face and said, "I'm going to where my sister is," to the young man who had just sat down across from the lighthouse keeper. Without saying a word, the downcast young man stared at the furrowed face of the boy. The girl suddenly buried her face in her hands and began to cry.

"Your father and your big sister, Kikuyo, still have work to do, but they'll be here soon. But your mother has probably been waiting a long time. Now, our biggest problem is what song shall we sing. I think we should all join hands this snowy morning and play going round and round the elderberry bush. We'll soon see your mother again. She's been waiting and is very worried."

"Yeah, so it's good I got on the ship," said the boy.

"Yes, but look ... look at the sky. Look at that beautiful river. During the summer, whenever I would sing *Twinkle, Twinkle, Little Star* at bedtime, I would look out the window and always see that foggy whiteness. It was very pretty and twinkled like that over there."

The crying girl wiped her eyes and looked outside. The young man gently spoke again to the children like a teacher giving a lesson.

"We'll be sad no more. We are traveling through this beautiful place and will soon be with God. It will be a bright, sweet-smelling place filled with wonderful people. Instead of us, all the people riding in the lifeboats will be saved. They are going home to their worried fathers and mothers who are waiting. We'll be there soon, so let's sing to cheer up."

As the young man patted the boy's damp, black hair and comforted him, his face brightened.

"Where are you from? What happened?" the lighthouse keeper finally managed to ask the young man. The young man laughed slightly.

"We ... we were on a ship. It hit an iceberg and sank. Two months ago, their father returned home to our country on urgent business, so we departed later. I was a college student working as a private tutor.

"On the twelfth day, today or maybe yesterday, the ship hit an iceberg. In an instant, it tilted and started sinking. The moonlight faintly lit everything, but the fog was extremely thick.

"Unfortunately, half of the lifeboats, the ones on the port side, were lost. So everyone couldn't get on, and even some of those boats sank. I became desperate and yelled to let the little ones on. People nearby immediately opened a path and prayed for the children. But from where we stood to the boats, there were still so many small children and parents. I didn't have the heart to push them aside. But I thought it was my duty to save these two somehow, so I pushed aside some children in front of me.

"Then I felt that it would be better for us all to go to the presence of God rather than to save them in that way. I thought this was truly for their happiness.

"I believed the crime against God would have been to save them by any means. But no matter how I looked at it, I couldn't do that. It tore me up inside to see mothers frantically kissing their children goodbye and mournful fathers stoically standing by as they let their children board the boats only for children.

"Some of those boats sank almost immediately, we hardened and became more resolute. These two hugged each other and waited for the boats that had just been launched to sink. Someone threw a life preserver, but it drifted away. I let go of the deck grating that I had been holding onto for dear life, and all three of us clung together.

"Then a voice from somewhere said number 306. In an instant, everyone was singing this song in many languages. Suddenly, we heard a deafening boom and fell into the water, but I held tight to these two as we were sucked into a whirlpool.

"That's all I remember until we got here. Their mother died a year ago. Hmm ... people were surely saved by the boats. Skilled sailors manned the oars and swiftly moved away from the ship."

Soft sighs and praying voices could be heard all around them. Giovanni and Campanella fuzzily recalled things they had forgotten, and their eyes welled with tears.

A dejected Giovanni's head hung low and he thought, Isn't that large ocean the Pacific? In the northern end of the ocean where icebergs flowed, everyone riding on the small boats being pummeled by those winds, frozen seawater, and fierce cold had to struggle. I feel so sorry for those unfortunate people. What could I do to make those people happy?

The lighthouse keeper had words of comfort for the young man.

"I don't know what is happiness. If there is some right path to follow after a horrible event, confronting and handling a crisis take you one step closer to true bliss."

"Ah, yes. Everyone desires various sorrows to reach true happiness," answered the young man as if in prayer.

The exhausted siblings were slumped in their seats asleep. Their previously shoeless feet now wore soft white shoes.

The train chugged along the banks of the glittering phosphorescent river. Through the window on the other side, they saw a field that resembled images from a magic lantern. They could see hundreds, maybe thousands, of large and small signal towers with survey flags marked with red points placed on the large ones. Many were grouped on all sides of the field. From time to time, faint objects resembling signal fires having a variety of shapes or hazy pale white fog from further away were launched one after another into a sky colored like beautiful balloon flowers. The graceful, transparent winds were filled with the scent of roses.

"Would you like one? This is probably the first time you've seen apples like these," said the lighthouse keeper holding several large, beautiful gold and crimson apples propped on his lap with both hands so they wouldn't fall off.

"Where did they come from? They are magnificent. Do apples like that grow here?" asked the surprised young man who forgetting himself stared at the apples held in the hands of the lighthouse keeper while squinting and tilting his head.

"Well, no. Please have one. Take it, please."

The young man took one and glanced at Giovanni and Campanella.

"Gentlemen, would you like one? Please take one."

Giovanni was a little annoyed at being

called a gentleman but said nothing. Campanella said, "Thank you."

When the young man passed an apple to each boy, Giovanni stood and said thank you.

The lighthouse keeper finally opened his arms and gently placed an apple on the laps of the young brother and sister.

"Thank you. Where are these grown? They're beautiful apples," said the young man while looking attentive.

"Of course, there is farming in these parts, but I promise to do something that I can do well alone. I am not really interested in farming. If you plant the seeds of your desire, you will rapidly become capable.

"The rice does not have a hull like near the Pacific. It's also ten times bigger and smells great. But there is no farming where you are going. Even the apples and the candies have no scraps, and their pores emit delicate pleasing scents that differ for each person."

The boy's eyes opened wide and he said, "Oh, I just saw my mother in a dream.

She was in a place with great big cabinets and lots of books. She saw me and held out her hands. She was smiling and laughing. But I guess I woke up when I said, 'Mother, I picked an apple and will give it to you. Oh, I'm still on that train from before.'"

"That apple is right there. This nice man gave it to you," said the young man.

"Thank you, Mister. Oh, Kaoru is still sleeping. I'll wake her up. Kaoru, wake up. Look, you have an apple. Wake up. Look."

Kaoru opened her eyes laughing, somewhat dazed, she rubbed her eyes, and then she saw the apple.

The boy had already devoured his apple like it was a slice of apple pie. He carefully peeled skin spiraling like a corkscrew emitted a gray color and evaporated as it dropped to the floor.

The two children carefully put the apples in their pockets.

A large bluish grove could be seen on the opposite shore downstream. The branches were heavy with ripe, bright red, round fruits. A very tall signal tower stood in the center of the grove. Unbelievably beautiful tones mixing orchestral bells and xylophones flowed by as if melted into or slipped between the incoming winds.

The young man trembled, appearing to rejuvenate his body.

They quietly listened to the music and watched a bright yellowish or light green field or a rug spread over one side of the field, and fog like white wax misted over the surface of the sun.

"Ooh, crows," cried out Kaoru sitting next to Campanella.

"They're not crows. They're all magpies," gently scolded Campanella. A laugh slipped out of Giovanni and embarrassed the girl. Many black crows had stopped and were standing still in lines above the bluish-white light of the field to receive the hazy light of the river.

"Well, the down on the back of a magpie's head grows straight back," interjected the young man.

The signal tower in the distant blue woods came right in the front of the train.

They could again hear the tune of hymn number 306 they listened to earlier. It sounds like the chorus of a multitude of people.

The young man's face suddenly paled. He stood and was about to go to the sound but reconsidered and returned to his seat. Kaoru touched a handkerchief to her face.

Even Giovanni's nose felt odd. At any time, anyone who sings that song gradually gains strength. Without thinking, both Giovanni and Campanella began to sing.

The blue woods of olive trees slowly faded behind them, still shining brightly on the far side of the invisible Milky Way. The mysterious sounds of the instruments flowing from there grew fainter, drowned out by the sounds of the train and the sounds of the wind.

"Ah! There are peacocks. There are peacocks."

"That wood is probably the Inn of the Lyres. I think the people in the large orchestra from long ago gathered in that forest and were surrounded by many blue peacocks."

"Yes, there were many," replied the girl.

As they got smaller and smaller, Giovanni saw the reflected light of the peacocks spreading their tails that at times rapidly shimmered in a bluish-white color above another forest resembling green buttons made from shells.

"So those sounds we heard before were the calls of peacocks," said Campanella to the girl.

She answered, "Yes, there were definitely about thirty."

Giovanni was struck by a sudden pang of sadness. He looked serious and about to say, "Campanella let's jump off here and have some fun."

However, Giovanni saw something mysterious further downstream. They were long, slender, slippery smooth, black bodies. They flew above the waters of the invisible Milky Way, advanced while shaped like bows, and seemed to be hidden by the waters.

He thought they were unusual and fascinated by them. The next time, they seemed to be much closer. Here and there, many of these strange, glossy black bodies flew out of the water and flipped over, and dove back in head first. They seemed to fly above the river like fish.

"What is that? Ta-chan. Look. There are so many. What are they?"

The sleepy boy rubbing his eyes stood up amazed.

"What are they?" said the young man who was also standing.

"Maybe, they're some kind of strange fish. What are they?"

"They're dolphins," answered Campanella, looking out the window.

"Dolphins. This is the first time I've seen them. But this isn't the ocean, right?"

"Dolphins don't just live in the ocean," said a mysterious low voice out of the blue.

The dolphins had a strange shape. The two fins seemed exactly like two motionless hands posed downward as they came flying out of the water, and their motionless heads bowed courteously as they dove into the water again. Waves of the invisible waters of the Milky Way rose up like flickering blue flames.

"Are dolphins fish?" the girl asked Campanella. The boy slept slumped in the seat. He must have been dead tired.

"Dolphins are not fish. They're mammals like whales," answered Campanella.

"You've seen a whale?"

"Yes, I have. But I could only see its head and black tail. It's spout looked exactly like it does in books."

"Whales are big, aren't they?"

"Yes, they are. Their children are about the size of dolphins."

"Yes. Yes. I saw that in Arabian Nights," said the girl very interested as she played with a small silver ring on her finger.

Giovanni thought, Campanella, sadly, I had already left and never saw the whale.

Giovanni had become unbearably angry, but he steeled himself, bit his lip, and looked out the window. The forms of the dolphins could no longer be seen outside the window and the river had branched in two.

A gigantic tower was erected in the center of a dark island. On top of the tower stood a lone man wearing baggy clothes and a red cap. Holding a red flag in one hand and a blue flag in the other, he was signaling while looking up at the sky.

Giovanni watched the man continuously wave the red flag, then suddenly dropped down the red flag behind him as if to hide it and raised the blue flag high and furiously waved it as an orchestra conductor. When he did that, he could hear sounds that sounded like a torrential rainstorm in the sky.

Flock after flock of pitch-black beings of some kind flew toward the river like bullets. Without realizing it, Giovanni thrust half his body out of the window for a better look. In the empty sky colored like beautiful balloon flowers, several tens of thousands of small birds in several flocks passed by ceaselessly singing.

"Birds are flying by," said Giovanni from outside the window.

"Oh!" said Campanella when he looked at the sky.

The man in the loose clothes on the tower suddenly raised the red flag and waved it frantically. Instantly, flocks of birds no longer passed through. Simultaneously, a bang sounded downstream, and a short time later, silence. The man in the red hat waved the blue flag in his signal hand and called out.

He could be clearly heard saying, "Now migrating birds. Now migrating birds."

The flocks of several tens of thousands of birds flew straight across the sky. The girl poked her face with beautiful glowing cheeks out of the window between the two boys' faces, and she looked up at the sky.

The girl tried to talk with Giovanni saying, "Wow, there are so many birds. The sky is so pretty," but he thought, Ugh, what a smart aleck, and stared straight ahead without saying a word. The girl let out a small sigh and returned to her seat saying no more. Campanella sadly pulled his head in from the window and looked at the map.

"Is that man training the birds?" softly asked the girl to Campanella.

"He is signaling the migrating birds. A flare is probably being sent up somewhere," Campanella answered a little unsure.

A hush fell over the train. Giovanni wanted to pull in his head, but he didn't want to be in a bright place. He stoically didn't move and whistled.

While pressing both hands to his fevered head, he thought, Why do I feel this sad? I should be enjoying this. I can see a small blue fire like smoke from a far-off shore. That place is really quiet and cold. When I look there, I feel comforted.

His eyes filled with tears. He only saw blurry white as the Milky Way faded into the distance and thought, Aah, I have no one to go anywhere with me anymore. It's really hard seeing Campanella happily talking with that girl.

The train gradually moved away from

the river and passed over the top of a cliff. The faraway cliff and a black cliff gradually grew taller as the train moved downstream along the river shore. Large stalks of corn could be seen. Their fronds withered into curls, and under the fronds, beautiful, large green leaves sprouted red hairs, and fruits like pearls. Their number gradually increased in rows between the cliff and the tracks.

Giovanni pulled his head in from the window and looked out the window across the aisle. He saw large corn stalks growing on most of that side until the ends of the fields at the horizon that met the gorgeous sky. The stalks swayed in the light winds. The tips of the splendid curled leaves were covered with diamond-like dewdrops that absorbed bright white light and emitted sparkling red and green lights.

"That's corn over there," Campanella said to Giovanni, but Giovanni looked listlessly at the field unable to feel better, and only said, "Seems so."

The train quieted, passed several signals and the lights of switches, and slowed to stop at a small depot.

The bluish-white clock on the front showed exactly two o'clock. The wind had died down and the train stopped. In the quiet field, the pendulum of the clock ticked precisely.

What sounded like a faint melody from strings flowed out between the sounds of pendulums from the ends of the far-off fields.

"It's the New World Symphony," said the girl in the other seat mumbled softly to herself and glanced at Giovanni.

The tall young man in black clothes and everyone else in the car had already seen the simple dream.

This place is so peaceful, but I don't feel any delight. Why do I feel so alone? Campanella has behaved horribly. We got on the train together, but he was only talking to that girl. This is so hard, thought Giovanni, who hid half of his face in his hand and stared out the window.

A whistle tooted like a glass flute, and

the train quietly accelerated. Campanella mournfully whistled *The Star Journey*.

"Yes, yes, this area is a harsh plateau," said a clear voice behind them from an older man who had just woken up.

"For corn, you use a pole to open a hole about two feet. If nothing is seeded there, nothing will grow."

"Really? There should be many more until the river?"

"Yes, yes, it's 2,000 feet to 6,000 feet to the river. Then there's a great ravine."

For no reason, Giovanni thought, Yes, that's probably the Great Plains in Colorado.

While her little brother slept leaning on his own chest, the girl's black pupils drifted to an enchanting object far away, and she was lost in thought. Campanella was still whistling dolefully. The boy whose complexion resembled an apple wrapped in silk looked to where Giovanni was gazing.

Instantly, the corn disappeared, and a gigantic black field spread out before them.

The distinct sounds of the New World Symphony welled up from the edge of the horizon. In the black field, a single Indian wearing the feathers of a white bird on his head and his chest and arms decorated with many jewels was gripping an arrow in a small bow and running at full speed after the train.

"Hey, it's an Indian! An Indian! Look Kaoru!"

The young man in the black suit also woke up.

Both Giovanni and Campanella stood.

"He's running toward us. He's coming this way. He's probably chasing us."

The young man, momentarily forgetting where he was, reached into his pocket, and stood up while saying, "No, he's not chasing the train. He's hunting or perhaps dancing."

The Indian seemed to be half dancing. First, his kicks and steps seemed economical and earnest. The bold white feathers instantly fell forward when the Indian stopped on a dime and swiftly shot an arrow into the sky.

A crane fell spinning from the sky. The Indian dashed off with both hands spread wide to catch it. He stood there laughing and smiling. The silhouette of him carrying the crane slowly faded into the distance until only the insulators of two telegraph poles continued to shine brilliantly. Then another cornfield appeared.

From the window, they realized the train was traveling on top of a very high cliff. At the bottom of the valley, the river widened and flowed brightly.

The old man said, "Yes, it drops down from here. From here on, the ride down to the water level is easy. The slope keeps the train from ever coming here from over there. We'll slowly speed up."

The train rapidly descended. When the tracks hit the edge of the cliff, the river peeked out brightly from below. Giovanni felt a little better.

The train passed in front of a small shack. Without realizing it, Giovanni cried out, startled by the sight of a lone unhappy child standing in front of the shack.

The train quickly gathered speed. The passengers held on tight to the benches while falling backward in the car. Surprising himself, Giovanni laughed with Campanella. The Milky Way flowed fiercely past the side of the train and twinkled at times. Scattered pink flowers bloomed on the pale red, dry riverbed. Finally, the train ran smoothly like it finally calmed down.

A flag decorated with a star shape and a pickaxe stood on the far shore.

"What sort of flag is that?" Giovanni asked.

"Hmm, I don't know. It's not on the map. There's an iron ship."

"Oh."

"Aren't they building a bridge?" asked the girl.

"Oh, that was an engineer's flag. It's a construction practice, but it looks like a military flag."

A little downstream near the far shore,

the invisible waters of the Milky Way shimmered and blasted high like a pillar accompanied by the sound of thunder.

"It was a cannon shot. An explosion!" shouted Campanella.

When the pillar of water disappeared, the glittering white bellies of large salmon and trout were flung into the air, traced round wheels, or dropped back into the water.

Giovanni, who felt a little like leaping up, said, "It's the Engineer's Battalion of the Sky. Trout can jump that high. I've never been on a pleasure trip like this. This is great."

"If you saw that trout up close, it's probably this big. There are so many fish in these waters."

"There are probably small fish, too," chimed in the girl.

"Maybe. There are probably big ones and small ones, but we can't see the small ones from this distance," Giovanni in a better mood, cheerfully answered the girl.

The boy looked out the window,

pointed, and shouted, "Those are the princes of the Gemini constellation."

Two princes who seemed to be made of small crystals stood side by side to the right on top of a small hill.

"They are the princes of the Gemini constellation," said the boy.

"Mother told me about them many times. Now, the two princes made of small crystals are standing right there," said the girl.

"Tell me about them. What do the Gemini princes do?"

The boy said, "I know. The Gemini princes play in the fields and fight the crows, I think."

The girl said, "No, that's not right. Mother said that on the shore of the Milky Way ..."

"Then a comet zooms by."

"No, no, Ta-chan. That's something else."

"So they're playing their flutes over there now, right?"

"Now we're going to the sea."

The girl said, "We can't. We've already been to the sea."

"Oh, yeah. I know. I'll tell you," said the boy.

* * *

The distant shore of the river had reddened.

Willow trees and the pitch-black transparency of the invisible waves of the Milky Way glowed red like twinkling needles. Large red flames burned in the field on the far-off shore, and black smoke rose high and scorched the frigid sky colored like balloon flowers. The fire burned with transparency redder than rubies and was more beautifully spellbinding than burning lithium.

Giovanni asked, "What's that fire? A fire burning that red is probably burning something."

"That's the fire of Scorpio," replied Campanella, again scrutinizing the map.

"Oh, I know about the fire of Scorpio," said the girl.

"What is the fire of Scorpio?" asked Giovanni.

"Scorpio was burnt to death, and that fire burns to this day. Father told me about that many times."

"Isn't a scorpion, an insect?"

"Yes, it is. But it's a good insect."

"Scorpions are not nice insects. I saw one preserved in alcohol at a museum. The teacher said that one sting from that stinger on its tail could kill you."

"That's true, but it's a good insect. Father said so. Long ago, a scorpion that lived on the Baldora Field killed and ate small insects to survive. One day, a weasel discovered him and wanted to eat him. The scorpion tried as hard as he could to escape. Just when it looked like the weasel was about to catch him, he suddenly tumbled into a well in his path. He tried but couldn't get out, and began to drown. At that moment, the scorpion recited this prayer.

I don't know how many lives I have taken. When it seemed like the weasel would take mine next, I tried to escape with all my might. And yet, I ended up here. Nothing is certain. Perhaps I should have given my body to the weasel without resistance. If I had, the weasel would live one more day. Well, God. Look into my heart. Please don't abandon this useless life. Somehow, the next time, use my body to bring happiness to others.

"All of a sudden, the scorpion's body burned up and became a magnificent, brilliant red flame that lit up the darkness of the night. And Father told me that it continues to burn to this day. That's what that fire is."

"Oh. I see it. The signal towers over there are shaped exactly like the scorpion."

Giovanni looked and saw three signal towers beyond the large fire that looked exactly like the legs of the scorpion and five signal towers lined up like the tail and stinger of the scorpion. The beautiful, radiant red fire of the scorpion burned silently and brilliantly.

As the fire receded behind them, everyone heard the sounds of whistles and the animated sounds of many people talking. The sounds were indescribably lively, like a medley of musical tones or the scents of flowers. It seemed like a nearby town was holding a celebration.

The boy, who had been asleep beside Giovanni until now, pointed out the window on the other side and yelled out, "Centaurus, bring us dewdrops."

There stood a deep blue spruce tree, like a Christmas tree, decorated with many small lights, like a gathering of thousands of fireflies.

"Oh, yes. Tonight is the Centaur Festival."

Campanella immediately said, "Oh, this is the Forest of the Centaurs."

[Original text missing]

***

"If I threw a ball at it, I would hit it," bragged the boy.

"We'll soon arrive at the Southern Cross. Get ready to get off," said the young man to the children.

The boy said, "I'm going to ride the train a little longer."

The girl seated next to Campanella started fidgeting and was anxious to stand, but she wasn't ready to say goodbye to Giovanni and Campanella.

"We must get off here," said the young man. He drew his lips tight and glared at the boy.

"No. I want to ride the train some more."

Unable to hold back, Giovanni said, "Ride with us. We have tickets that can go anywhere."

"But we must get off here, because this is where we go to Heaven," said the girl sadly.

"Is it okay not to go to Heaven? My

teacher said that this place is better than Heaven."

"But Mother's also going there, and God is there."

"That kind of God is a false god."

"Your God is a false god."

"No, that's not so."

"What kind of God is your God?" asked the young man while laughing.

"I really don't know. But it's not that, there is one true God."

"Of course, there is one true God."

"Oh, one God is the true God."

"Isn't that so? I will pray that you will meet us now before the true God," said the young man as he humbly clasp his hands together.

The girl did the same. Everyone was unhappy about their parting. Their complexions looked a little pale. Giovanni's voice broke like he was about to cry as he said, "A little longer would be nice? But soon we'll be at the Southern Cross."

It was time. A cross studded with blue and orange lights stood like a tree glittering in the center of the river far downstream in the invisible Milky Way. A ring of bluish-white clouds hung above like lights. The inside of the train was bustling. Everyone stood up and began to pray as they had before the Northern Cross.

Only the playful voices of children, as though they were tossing gourds, here and there and indistinct, deep simple sighing sounds could be heard. The cross slowly filled the front of the window and was gently encircled by a ring of bluish white clouds like the fruit surrounding an apple core.

Everyone's bright, happy voices resounded, "Hallelujah! Hallelujah!"

An unseen, clear bracing voice could be heard from far off in the sky, far off in the cold sky. The train slowed amid many signals and electric lights and stopped before the cross.

"Well, it's time," said the young man pulling on the boy's hand. His sister fixed her collar and shoulders and slowly walked to the exit.

Night on the Milky Way Railroad

The girl turned to the boys and said, "Well, this is goodbye."

"Bye," Giovanni brusquely replied to keep from crying.

The girl's eyes opened wide with vivid heartache and turned again to the boys, then left without speaking. The train was more than half empty and desolate; an air of sorrow swept in.

Looking out, everyone had formed a simple line and kneeled in prayer on the shore of the Milky Way before the cross. The boys spotted a lone divine figure dressed in white extending a hand over the invisible waters of the Milky Way toward them. But the glass whistle had already sounded, and the train was moving off.

A silver fog rolled in from downstream and blocked their view. Many walnut trees with brilliant glittering leaves stood in the fog. Only the cute face of an electric squirrel holding a golden halo flitted in and out of view through the fog.

* * *

When the fog lifted, alongside the track was a road lined with small lights like a highway. As the boys passed in front of the lights, a small dark red light flicked off and lit up again like a polite greeting.

Giovanni glanced back to see the cross had become tiny and seemed to be truly suspended unchanged in his heart. He could not tell whether the girl, the young man, and the others were still kneeling on the white shore or left in some unknown direction to Heaven.

He took a deep breath.

"Campanella, it's just us again. We'll go as far as we can. Like that scorpion, it wouldn't bother me if my body burned one hundred times if that would truly bring happiness to all."

"Yes, me too," said Campanella as genuine tears welled up.

Giovanni said, "But what is true happiness?"

"I don't know," said Campanella, preoccupied.

"We'll find out together," exclaimed

Giovanni filled with emotion and a surge of renewed strength.

Evading the subject, Campanella pointed to a part of the Milky Way and said, "Look over there, it's the Coalsack Nebula. That dark hole over there."

Giovanni looked and was startled by the sight. A huge, gaping black hole was in a part of the Milky Way. How deep is the bottom? What's inside? No matter how much he rubbed his eyes and looked, he saw nothing and his eyes only ached. He said, "I wouldn't be afraid in that vast darkness. I would search for true happiness for everyone. We could go anywhere together."

"Yes, we should go. That field is probably beautiful. Everyone is gathered there. That is where Heaven truly is. Oh, my mother is over there," cried out Campanella, pointing to a beautiful distant field he could see from the window.

Giovanni looked but only saw a faint white smoke and couldn't imagine what Campanella was talking about.

His despair was indescribable. When

he looked there a little distracted, he saw two telegraph poles standing on the far shore linked by red crosspieces to tie together the arms from both poles.

Giovanni said, "Campanella, let's go there," and turned to him. His seat was empty. Only his impression was left on the shiny black velvet.

Giovanni shot up like a bullet, leaned far out the window so no one could hear, and screamed with all his might and cried in grief.

He thought that everything around him had become black.

"Why are you crying? Look over here," said that voice Giovanni heard from time to time. The voice came from behind him and sounded like a soothing cello.

Startled, Giovanni turned, brushing away his tears. Sitting in Campanella's seat was a man with a thin, pale face and wearing a large black hat. He was kindly laughing and holding a large book.

"Where did your friend go? Well,

tonight he's gone very far away. It would be pointless to search for Campanella."

"But why? Campanella and I were going to go forward together."

"Ah, yes. Everyone thinks that way. But you can't go together. Everyone is Campanella. They're anyone you have met, anyone who ate apples with you many times, or who rode the train. Therefore, as you thought earlier, it is good to search for the most happiness for all and to quickly go there with everyone. Only there could you go with Campanella forever."

"Yes, I must do that. It's good for me to seek that."

"Yes, I too am seeking that. You are holding tight to your ticket. You must study single-mindedly. Perhaps chemistry would be good for you. Water is known to be composed of oxygen and hydrogen. Who doubts that now? Experiment and see that this is true. Long ago, there were disputes over whether water could be made from mercury and salt, or mercury and sulfur.

"Everyone says that his God is the true

God, but tears probably overflow even for things done to people who believe in another God. We should debate the good parts and the bad parts of ourselves. The struggle is probably not over.

"If you study hard and experiment, and divide ideas into true ideas and false ideas, if you determine the experimental method, belief and science become the same.

"Look at this book. All right? This is a dictionary of geography and history. This page in this book is about the geography and history around 2200 BC. If you look closely, this is not 2200 BC. What is written are the geography and the history that everyone believed around 2200 BC.

"Therefore, this single page is in one volume of a geography and history book. All right. What is written here is true for the most part around 2200 BC. If you search, the proof will be revealed little by little. But think a bit about what will happen ... well that ... that is on the next page.

"In the year 1000 BC, both geography

and history would be different. This is that time. Don't make a face. We feel our bodies, thoughts, the Milky Way, trains, and history. So look there, quietly look with me into your heart. All right?"

He raised one finger and then gently lowered it. As he did so, in a flash, Giovanni understood everything, himself, his thoughts, the train, the scholar, the Milky Way, and it slowly disappeared, flashed again, then disappeared again. When it flashed again, he saw the whole world start empty, be endowed with history, then all of it disappear and become empty again, and then be forgotten. This cycle accelerated and in an instant became as it was before.

"All right? So your experiment is to understand everything from the beginning to the end of these fragmented thoughts. That is difficult, but it's only good that way. Oh, look. You can see Perseus over there. You have to unravel Perseus' chain."

A bluish-white beacon emerged from the pitch black horizon like daylight and lit up the interior of the train. The beacon continued to radiate high in the sky.

"That is the Magellan galaxy. I am searching for true happiness for me, for my mother, for Campanella, for everyone."

Giovanni bit his lip, looked at the Magellanic Cloud, and stood still. For the happiness of all!

Giovanni thought he heard the cello-like voice say, "Well, hold on tight to that ticket. You must stride straight through the fires and the rough waves in the real world, not on a dream railroad. You must not lose that ticket, the only one of its kind in the Milky Way."

Far off in the Milky Way where the wind was blowing, Giovanni saw himself standing on a grassy hill. He also heard the approach of the quiet footsteps of Professor Brucaniro from a distance.

"Thank you. I have conducted a great experiment. Earlier, I thought that I wanted to experiment with sending my thoughts to someone from a long distance away at this quiet location. All of your words are in my notebook. Well, go home now and rest. You should push forward with the determination you had in this dream. In the future, please consult with me at any time about anything."

"I will definitely push forward. I am seeking true happiness," said Giovanni in a determined voice.

"Well then, goodbye. This is the ticket from before."

The Professor put the small, folded piece of green paper in Giovanni's pocket. Then, his figure disappeared past the Pillar of the Wheel of Heaven.

Giovanni ran straight down the hill. As he ran, he became aware of a heavy weight rattling in his pocket. When he stopped in the forest to investigate, two large gold coins were wrapped in that mysterious green ticket from Heaven he had seen in his dream.

"Thank you, Professor. Mom, I'm going to get the milk right now," yelled Giovanni as he took off running. But in an instant, he was choked up by emotion, it was something new, an unspeakable sadness.

The Lyra constellation had traveled far to the west and stretched its legs as in the dream.

* * *

Giovanni opened his eyes. He was tired and had fallen asleep in the grass on the hill. His chest felt strangely hot, and cold tears had run down his cheeks.

Giovanni sprang to his feet. In the town below, many lights were woven together as before, but they seemed to be burning hotter.

The Milky Way of his dream became a dim white haze on the deep black horizon to the south. On its right, the red star of Scorpio twinkled splendidly. The position of the whole sky seemed to have changed very little.

Giovanni dashed down the hill. He worried about his mother who was waiting and had not eaten dinner. He ran through the black forest, each step pounding the ground. He ran around the dull white gate of the pasture and stood again at the entrance to the dark cow barn. Someone else seemed to be there. A truck that wasn't there before was loaded with two barrels.

"Good evening," called out Giovanni.

"Yes." A man wearing baggy white trousers popped out.

"How can I help you?"

"Our milk wasn't delivered today."

"Oh, I'm sorry."

The man went back inside and returned with a bottle of milk. While handing it over to Giovanni, he said laughing, "I'm really sorry. This afternoon I was a bit careless and left the gate open. The calves got loose and went right over to their mothers and drank half the milk."

"Oh, wow. Well, thank you. Goodnight."

"Goodnight. Sorry again."

"No, no, it's okay."

Giovanni went out the gate of the pasture holding the bottle of warm milk in both hands.

In no time, he was passing a tree-lined street that opened into a large avenue. A little further up, the streets formed a cross. Just off the street to the right, in a haze in front of the night sky stood the beams of the large bridge jutting out over the river where Campanella and the others went earlier to float their lights.

But now, about seven or eight women were gathered in front of a store at the street corner forming a cross. They were speaking softly while looking toward the bridge. He could see many lights on the bridge.

Giovanni wondered why a chill swept over him. He called out to some people nearby, "What happened?"

One replied, "Some children fell into the river."

All at once, they looked at Giovanni. He ran furiously toward the bridge. The bridge was crammed with so many people he couldn't see the water. Policemen in white uniforms were there, too.

Giovanni got to the wide riverbed quickly, as if he jumped from the foot of the bridge.

Many lights lining the water's edge of the riverbed were busily being raised and lowered. Seven or eight fires were moving on the dark riverbank on the far shore. The river had no gourd lights floating in the center but was a gently flowing grayness accompanied by little sound.

One group stood in a distinct blackness on the furthest downstream sandbar of the river. Giovanni ran there with heavy steps. Maruso who had been with Campanella earlier was there. Maruso ran toward Giovanni and said, "Giovanni, Campanella went in the river."

"Why? When?"

"You see, Zanelli, tried to push the lighted gourd from a boat into the flowing water. But the boat wobbled and he fell in. Campanella immediately jumped in and pushed Zanelli to the boat. Zanelli grabbed onto Kato. But after that, we never saw Campanella again."

"Everyone's been looking for him."

"Yes, everyone came in a flash. Campanella's father came, too. But we still haven't found him. They took Zanelli home."

Giovanni went to where everybody was waiting. The students and the townspeople had gathered around Campanella's father, a man with a pale, sharp chin. Dressed in black and standing ramrod straight, he was carefully checking the watch he held in his left hand.

Everyone was intently staring at the river. No one said a word. Giovanni's legs were shaking. Many acetylene lamps used for fishing were busily coming and going. Small glittering standing waves could be seen in the black waters of the flowing river.

The river downstream greatly mirrored and resembled the waterless sky of the Milky Way.

Giovanni couldn't help thinking Campanella already left that Milky Way.

But while someone somewhere among the waves was saying, "I'm a strong swimmer," some seemed to feel that Campanella had gotten out, or that he was standing on some bank no one knew about and waiting for help. But Campanella's father abruptly said with certainty,

"It's over. If he fell in forty-five minutes ago, ..."

Before he realized it, Giovanni ran up to and was standing in front of the Professor. He was about to tell the Professor that he knows where Campanella went and he had been with him, but he choked up and said nothing. The Professor greeted Giovanni and fixed his gaze on him, then politely said, "You are Giovanni, aren't you? Thank you for your help tonight."

Giovanni bowed in silence.

"Has your father returned?" asked the Professor tightly gripping his watch.

"No," said Giovanni shaking his head.

"I wonder what happened. The day before yesterday, I received great news. I thought they'd arrive today. The ship's probably been delayed. Giovanni, please bring your classmates to my house after school tomorrow to play."

As he spoke, the Professor directed his gaze downstream where the Milky Way filled the sky.

Giovanni was bursting with emotions. Without a word, he left the Professor and hurried to take the milk to his mother. He thought she would know about his father's return and ran at full speed along the riverbed to town.

Credits

Japanese source text:
Aozora Bunko. Miyazawa, Kenji. "Ginga Tetsudo no Yoru," (in Japanese). Accessed July 18, 2014.
Input by: Kouno Motoko
Revised by: Tsuchiya Takashi

https://www.aozora.gr.jp/cards/000081/card43737.html

Cover image derived from:
　Milky Way railway watercolor stock illustration by marumaru

About the Author

Kenji Miyazawa was born August 27, 1896 and died September 21, 1933. He was a Japanese poet and writer of fables. His writings were rooted in Buddhism and country life. During his life, his work was mostly unknown and gained notice only after his death through the efforts of Shinpei Kusano and other friends. He quickly became a favorite author in Japan and remains popular to this day. In addition to *Night on the Milky Way Railroad*, other beloved Miyazawa stories are *The Restaurant of Many Orders* and *Gauche the Cellist*.

Printed in Great Britain
by Amazon

40926302R10066